Whistling Dixie

MARCIA VAUGHAN

Whistling Dixie

Illustrated by Barry Moser

HarperCollins*Publishers*

ONE MORNING as Dixie Lee was whistling a lively tune and hunting for crawdads in Hokey Pokey Swamp, she found something to show her mama.

"Look, Mama, I found this little bitty gator. It's lost all its brothers and sisters. I 'spect I'll keep it for a pet."

"Mercy me, an *alligator*, Dixie Lee? We've got no place to put an alligator, child!"

"We can keep it down yonder in the well, Mama."

"Dixie Lee, you know I keep my churn down the well."

"I know, Mama. And this gator can swallow up any churn turners that slide down the well to drink up your buttermilk."

Dixie Lee's mama was none too fond of churn turners. Those slimy creatures could come oozing out of the mud in Hokey Pokey Swamp and guzzle up a churnful of buttermilk as easy as spitting off a bridge.

"All right, Dixie Lee. You can keep that gator down the well, but I don't know what your grand-pappy's going to say when he gets home. Now take this basket and go gather up a dozen eggs. And no more critters. Promise?"

"Cross my heart and hope to sit on a splinter." Dixie Lee grinned and went whistling off into the tall grass.

By the time Dixie Lee had filled her basket with eggs, she'd found something else to show her mama.

"Look, Mama, I found this slithery snake in the grass. It was all alone. I 'spect I'll keep it for a pet."

"Mercy me, a *snake*, Dixie Lee? We've got no place to put a snake, child."

"We could keep it in the gomper jar, Mama."

"But your grandpappy pops his gompers in that jar while he's snoozing."

"I know, Mama. And this snake can make sure no bogeyman comes sneaking in to steal 'em."

Dixie Lee's mama knew there was nothing in the whole wide world a bogeyman liked better than gompers. He'd string all those teeth together and make a necklace that jingled and jangled as he went prowling through the swamp at night.

"All right, Dixie Lee," sighed Mama. "You can keep that snake in the gomper jar, but I don't know what your grandpappy's going to say when he gets home. Now listen here, go hang up all this washing and no more critters. *Promise?*"

"Cross my heart and hope to swallow a frog," Dixie said with a wink.

By and by, as Dixie Lee was pegging up the wash, she found something else to show her mama.

"Look, Mama, I found this little hoot owl stuck in the branches of a tree. She's awful pretty. I 'spect I'll keep her for a pet."

"Mercy me, an *owl*, Dixie Lee? For sure and certain we've got no place to put an owl, child."

"We can keep her up the chimney, Mama."

"Now why in blue blazes would we want an owl up our chimney?"

"To keep the mist sisters from floating down and leaving a parcel of bad luck behind."

Dixie Lee's mama knew the one thing the mist sisters were afraid of was an owl. 'Cause if an owl asked them *whoo* they were, they'd have to tell the truth. Then all their magic would melt away like butter on a hot waffle.

"All right, Dixie Lee. Keep that owl up the chimney. But I really don't know what your grand-pappy's going to say when he gets home. Now it's off to cut cattails for tickly-tail stew."

Just as Dixie Lee and her mama disappeared into the swamp, down the road came Grandpappy, feeling thirsty as a jump bug in June. He reckoned he'd wet his whistle with a cool drink of buttermilk from the well.

No sooner had he reached down into the well than *SNAP SNAP CRACK!*

Spinning round like a top, Grandpappy went hooting and hollering and hotfooting it inside so fast, he had to lie right down and catch his breath. 'Course he popped out his teeth and plunked them in the gomper jar without looking.

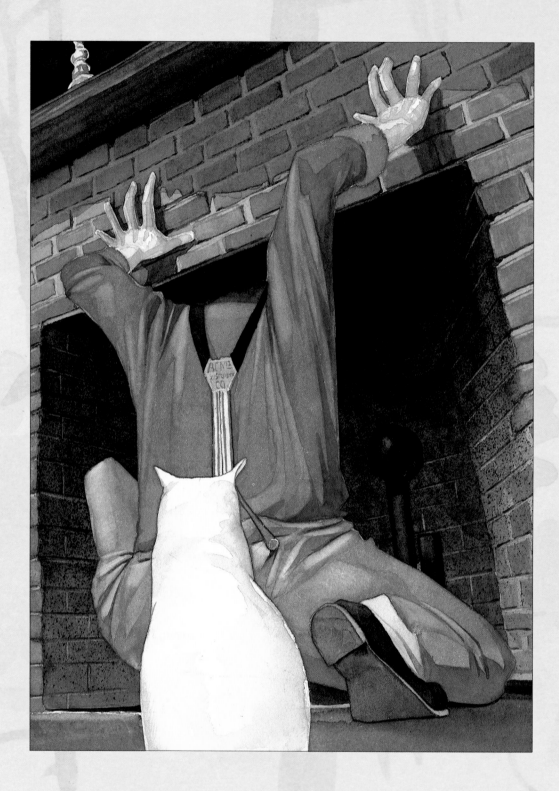

"JUMPING JIMINY!" howled Grandpappy, louder than a bee-stung bull.

"Whooz-that? Whooz-that?" hooted the owl.

"Tarnation, if that don't sound like somebody hiding up the chimney," declared Grandpappy, poking his head so far up inside, it stuck tight as a cork in a jug of molasses.

He stayed stuck, too, until Dixie Lee and her mama came home and yanked him out by the seat of his britches.

"Out they go!" sputtered Grandpappy. "Every one of them no-good critters goes back to Hokey Pokey Swamp at sunup, you hear?"

That very night, as the moon was peeking up over the hills, out of Hokey Pokey Swamp oozed five slimy churn turners. Slithering and squirming, slinking and sliding, they headed straight for the well to guzzle up all Mama's buttermilk.

Closer and closer they squirmed. Up and onto the well they turned. Down and into the well they wormed.

SNAP SNAP CRACK! Quicker than you can swat a skeeter, that gator shot up, swallowed them, and spit out their slimy green tails. Patooie!

Later, as the moon was sitting way up in the treetops, out of Hokey Pokey Swamp stomped the bogeyman. The necklace of teeth dangling round his neck jingled and jangled as he slipped through the window to steal Grandpappy's gompers.

Closer and closer he sneaked. Up to the bedside he creaked. And into that jar he jammed his furry fist.

FLICKER FLICKER SNICKER! That snake began tickling the bogeyman's hairy hand with its tongue.

"Ho-ooooooh!" The bogeyman started to laugh. He laughed until tears poured out of his hairy eyeballs. He laughed till tears rolled down his hairy face. That bogeyman laughed so hard, he turned into a puddle on the floor and dried up. All that was left was his necklace of teeth.

Not long after, as the moon was sailing high in the blue-black sky, three mist sisters rose up out of Hokey Pokey Swamp. Twisting and twirling, swishing and swirling, they drifted toward the house to turn good luck into bad.

Closer and closer they curled. Up the walls they whirled. Across the roof they furled. Down the chimney they swirled.

"Whooz-that? Whooz-that?" hooted the owl.

"It's the mist sisters," wailed the three. Melting into a green fog, they floated away forever, leaving only good luck behind.

Next morning, as the sun was trading places with the moon, Grandpappy crawled out of bed.

The first thing he found was the bogeyman's string of teeth on the floor. The second was the churn turners' tails by the well. And the third was enough good luck to last a lifetime.

That's when Mama and Grandpappy realized what good critters Dixie Lee had brought home after all.

And that's for sure!

For my family, who is more fun
than a tote sack full of tickle bugs!
—M V

For my friend, Eric Carle
—B M

*Special thanks to Erin who kept it, Willa who accepted it, Barry who
brought it to life, and Susan who saw it through!*
—M V

Whistling Dixie
Text copyright © 1995 by Marcia Vaughan
Illustrations copyright © 1995 by Barry Moser

Library of Congress Cataloging-in-Publication Data
Vaughan, Marcia K.
  Whistling Dixie / Marcia Vaughan ; illustrated by Barry Moser.
    p.   cm.
  *Summary: Dixie Lee brings home an alligator, a snake, and an owl
as pets to protect her family from spooky creatures such as the churn
turners, the bogeyman, and the mist sisters.*
  ISBN 0-06-021030-3. — ISBN 0-06-021029-X (lib. bdg.)
  [1. Swamps—Fiction.   2. Pets—Fiction.   3. Animals—Fiction.
4. Supernatural—Fiction.]   I. Moser, Barry, ill.   II. Title.
PZ7.V452Wh   1995   *91-45831*
[E]—dc20   *CIP*
                                                             AC

Design and typography by Barry Moser

2 3 4 5 6 7 8 9 10
❖
First Edition